# Characters in the Story

VISHNU ~ Vish-noo
*One of the three major gods in Hinduism,
Vishnu is the Preserver of the Universe*

KING DASHRATHA ~ Dash-ra-tha
*The King of the great city, Ayodhya*

BHARATA ~ Bha-ra-tha
*The son of Kaikeyi, a stepbrother of Rama*

RAMA ~ RAA-ma
*The son of King Dashratha
and the hero of* The Ramayana

LAKSHMANA~ Lak-sh-ma-na
*Rama's younger brother,
son of King Dashratha*

KING JANAKA ~ Jan-a-ka
*The father of Princess Sita*

JATAYU ~ Ja-TAI-u
*The King of the Birds*

SITA ~ See-Ta
*Daughter of King Janaka,
who becomes the wife of Rama*

HANUMAN ~ Han-oo-man
*The God of the Wind*

KAIKEYI ~ Ka-ee-kayee
*King Dashratha's second wife,
stepmother to Rama*

RAVANA ~ RAA-van-a
*The Demon King of Lanka*

*To the memory of my father, on whose lap I first heard* The Ramayana *under the Nairobi night-sky — J. V.*
*For Sarwat — N. M.*

Barefoot Books
3 Bow Street
Cambridge, MA 02138

Text copyright © 2002 by Jatinder Verma
Illustrations copyright © 2002 by Nilesh Mistry

The moral right of Jatinder Verma to be identified as the author and
Nilesh Mistry to be identified as the illustrator of this work has been asserted

This book has been printed on 100% acid-free paper
The illustrations were prepared in gouache on 140lb watercolor paper
Design by Jennie Hoare, England
Typeset in Minion Regular 14.5pt
Color separation by Bright Arts, Singapore
Printed and bound in Hong Kong by South China Printing Co. Ltd.

1 3 5 7 9 8 6 4 2

Library of Congress Cataloging-in-Publication Data

Verma, Jatinder Nath, 1954-
  Rama, Sita and the story of Divaali / retold by Jatinder Verma ;
illustrated by Nilesh Mistry.
    p. cm.
Summary: Retells the Hindu tale of a heroic prince and his bride who are
separated by the demon prince Ravana until the Monkey Army of Hanuman,
god of the wind, helps them. Includes facts about Divaali, the festival
celebrating Råama and Såitåa's return to their kingdom.
Includes bibliographical references and index.
  ISBN 1-84148-936-0
  1. Råama (Hindu deity)⁻Juvenile literature. 2. Såitåa (Hindu
deity)⁻Juvenile literature. [1. Råama (Hindu deity) 2. Såitåa (Hindu
deity) 3. Folklore⁻India. 4. Divali.] I. Mistry, Nilesh, ill. II.
Våalmåiki. Råamåayaòna. III. Title.
  BL1139.25 .V47 2002
  294.5'2113--dc21
                                                            2002000204

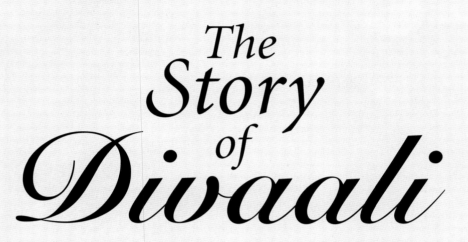

# The
# Story
# of
# Divaali

retold by
**Jatinder Verma**

illustrated by
**Nilesh Mistry**

**Barefoot Books**
*Celebrating Art and Story*

*I*n the beginning, long ago, long before you were born, Vishnu, the king of the gods, lay asleep on his giant hooded cobra. His booming snores created the rising and falling tides in the oceans and the rising and setting of the sun in the skies.

One day, a humming and popping noise like a swarm of bees buzzed around his head, and disturbed his sleep. He tossed this way and that, trying to make the noise go away. When it

did not, he first opened one eye to see what the trouble was, and then the other. There in front of him were three thousand, three hundred and thirty-three gods, all talking at once.

"Oh, great Vishnu," cried the three thousand, three hundred and thirty-three, "while you have been sleeping, darkness has crept upon the Earth. The demon Ravana's breath has eclipsed the sun. You must go down to Earth, or soon the heavens themselves will be dark!"

Vishnu bowed his head, and when he looked up, there was a twinkle in his eye. "Tell me," he said, "is there anyone on Earth who is, at this very moment, making sacrifices to the gods for good fortune?"

"Dashratha!" cried the three thousand, three hundred and thirty-three gods. "King Dashratha of Ayodhya is performing a huge sacrifice, to plead for a son."

Vishnu closed his eyes, and at that instant became a whirling column of fire. And the fire began to move, down, down, down, until it hit the ground where King Dashratha was performing his sacrifice. And when the fire touched the ground, there arose, through the flames, the most handsome prince imaginable, with an immense bow slung on his right shoulder and a single arrow in his left hand.

The prince stepped out of the fire, bowed his head before King Dashratha and, touching his feet, said, "Father, I am Rama, your eldest son." The king looked speechlessly at the miraculous young man, whose body shone as if flames danced upon his skin.

The high priest turned to the king and said, "Your Majesty, your son must have a wife, for he is to become king in his own right one day."

"A wife?" the king said. "When there is darkness all around, what would a wife bring?"

"Perhaps a light in the gloom that clouds our skies," replied the wise priest.

Then the king asked the high priest who would make a suitable wife for his son, Rama.

"The beautiful Princess Sita, daughter of King Janaka," said the high priest immediately. And so Prince Rama set off straight away for the kingdom of Mithila, where King Janaka ruled.

When they reached the court of King Janaka, Rama and the high priest found themselves in the midst of a crowd of hundreds and thousands of handsome young noblemen. Each one had come, like Rama, to win the beautiful Princess Sita for himself. And when Rama set eyes on Sita, he fell in love instantly, and knew that he must take her home as his bride.

King Janaka faced the crowd. When everyone was silent, he spoke out. "Here, before you, lies the great bow of Shiva. First

with your left hand, you must lift it up. And then, you must string it. And then, you must set this great arrow, also given to me by Shiva the Destroyer, on the bowstring. And finally, without looking at it directly, you must shoot the arrow straight into the eye of the fish which spins on the wheel set high above our heads. He amongst you who can do all these things will win my precious daughter for his bride and have my blessing."

At his words a murmur rose in the great hall. Some of the young men bowed their heads and turned away because the challenge King Janaka had set was too difficult. Others puffed out their chests and went up to the bow of Shiva, expecting to be able to lift it easily. One by one, each fell flat on his back, without moving the bow even an inch. And so the day wore on, and the bow lay unmoved at the Princess Sita's feet.

All of a sudden, there was a thunderclap; the sky darkened, and there in the doorway to Janaka's palace stood Ravana, the Demon King of Lanka. Without a word, he strode through the palace, scattering the crowd as he went. He glanced once at the Princess Sita, and then bent down to lift the great bow of Shiva. It did not budge. With a furious bellow, which shook the palace, he tried again — and fell smack to the ground. A great shout of laughter burst through the hall. Even the beautiful Sita, peeping anxiously through her veil, could not suppress her shy smile at his failure. This did not go unnoticed. Ravana turned to her and growled, "Soon, a day will come when that smile will become a stranger to you, Princess Sita!" And, muttering horribly, the Demon King stormed out.

Then up stood Prince Rama. Without taking his eyes from the princess's face, he lifted the great bow with his left hand, strung it effortlessly, and shot the arrow straight into the middle of the eye of the fish circling overhead.

A smile of delight lit up Sita's face, and a roar of applause filled the hall of King Janaka. "I have returned your smile to you, Princess Sita," said Rama joyfully.

Then Sita, with gentle hands, placed her garland of flowers around Rama's neck. "This is truly a marriage made in heaven," declared King Janaka, and from the roof of his great hall, hundreds and thousands of sweet-smelling jasmine petals fell to the floor.

A joyous King Dashratha greeted Rama and Sita on their return to the kingdom of Ayodhya, and the land was filled with festivities at the news that Rama had won Sita for his bride.

But, in a shadowy state room in the palace, there was one who was not happy at all — Rama's stepmother, Kaikeyi, King Dashratha's second wife.

Kaikeyi sulked alone in her room. "Now that Rama has a wife," she brooded, "a son will follow soon. And when that happens, my own son, Bharata, will lose the chance of becoming King of Ayodhya. It is a mother's duty to get the best for her son and I would fail in my duty if I did not try to make sure my own Bharata becomes king!"

Kaikeyi sent for King Dashratha. So exhilarated was he that, on seeing his queen sitting alone, he said, "My queen, why this long face? Come, ask me for anything you desire and it will be yours! For today is a day like no other! Come, let me make you even happier than I am today."

"Do you promise?" asked Kaikeyi.

"I promise," replied Dashratha. "What I say will come to pass. So come, my queen, tell me how I can make you happy."

So Kaikeyi told King Dashratha that her son Bharata, not Rama, had to become king after Dashratha, and that Rama must be sent away into exile for fourteen years.

When Dashratha heard these words, his heart turned to stone and he collapsed on the floor. Rama rushed into the room and, seeing his father lying on the floor, looked up at Kaikeyi in horror.

"He made me a promise. Now he wants to take it back," said his stepmother.

"I will fulfill any promise made by my father," replied Rama, with dignity.

"Then you must leave for the forest immediately, so that my son Bharata may become king." A gleam of malice sparkled in Kaikeyi's eyes as she spoke.

Rama turned to Dashratha who was now weeping. "Father," said Rama, "please don't be sad. I am proud to carry out your promise. Sons are born to obey their parents, so let joy fill your heart again, knowing that the word you have given will not be broken."

So Rama left the palace of Dashratha. As he walked toward the city gates, he heard a soft footfall behind him, and the sweet voice of Sita saying, "Rama, my husband, how can you think of leaving without me? I am the companion of your days, and wherever your fate leads, I shall be with you."

Then Lakshmana, Rama's younger brother, ran up. "You cannot go without me!" he cried breathlessly. "It is a brother's duty to help his brother." So the three of them continued on their way.

They came to the bank of the great River Ganges, and as the boatman ferried them across the water, a great silence fell upon the three travelers as they watched the kingdom of Ayodhya disappear on the horizon and the forest of Dandaka rise ahead, dark and full of mystery.

Now Sita turned to Rama and said, "We have left one life and are about to begin another. We must change our clothes." Rama and Lakshmana stripped bark from the trees, which

Sita made into clothes for the three of them. And all their jewelry, their fine silks and other garments that they had worn as princes and princesses of a great kingdom, they gave to the boatman as payment for his services.

Rama and Lakshmana found a clearing in the forest and built a small hut made of bark and covered with banana leaves. Every morning, Rama and Lakshmana would leave the hut to hunt for food, while Sita stayed near it gathering berries and herbs and cooking as best she could. Where once they had had hundreds of servants to look after their every need, now they had only themselves. But all three of them enjoyed this new adventure, not missing for a single day the pleasures of the palace they had been forced to leave.

Thus the years passed.

One day, when Rama and Lakshmana had returned from their morning's hunting and were just finishing their first meal of the day, Sita saw a little golden deer eating leaves from a small bush. She let out a sigh of longing and admiration.

Turning to Rama she said, "Have you ever seen an animal more beautiful? Oh, Rama, please bring that deer to me! When you go out hunting, I am all alone. This deer will be my companion."

Rama was not happy about leaving Sita, but seeing the plea in her eyes, he decided to make her wish come true. Picking up his bow and arrow, he told Lakshmana to stay behind with Sita, while he went to catch the deer. As Rama walked toward the deer, it suddenly turned and leaped over the bush, running deep into the forest. Rama gave chase, running as fast as he could. Soon, both of them were hidden from the eyes of Sita and Lakshmana.

As Rama chased the deer, he found that whenever he drew near it would slip away. Deeper and deeper into the forest the deer took Rama, until even the sun could not send its rays through the leaves. At last, Rama grew tired of the chase. He picked up his bow and shot an arrow, aiming to wound the creature's leg and slow it down. Just as the arrow struck the deer, a voice that sounded exactly like Rama's rang out through the forest: "Sita, Sita! Help me! Lakshmana, come quickly!"

Sita heard the cry and said, "Lakshmana! Rama is hurt! You must go and help him!" but Lakshmana refused.

"That is not Rama's true voice," he answered. "The deer was a demon, sent to trick me into leaving you."

But Sita would not give him any peace. "If you won't go to help him, I'll go myself!"

Lakshmana glared at her. "Very well, I'll go and chase your illusion," he said. "But whatever you do," he told Sita, "you must not step outside this circle." Then he took an arrow and drew a circle on the ground around the hut. "So long as you stay inside this circle, no harm will come to you, and I can still obey Rama's command." Then Lakshmana ran off into the forest.

Lakshmana's departure did not go unnoticed. Within

minutes, an old man appeared near the hut. Dressed in torn and dirty clothes, he could hardly stand, and had to support himself on a crooked stick. "Is anyone there?" he called. "Help, please help me." Sita came out of the hut and greeted the old man. "How hungry I am," moaned the old man, "and so tired and thirsty, too. Is there any food to eat in the house, and water to drink?" Quickly, Sita went back into the hut and brought out a bowl of rice and a pot of water. The old man walked toward her, but as his foot crossed the line Lakshmana had drawn on the ground, a huge wall of flame rose from the ground, encircling the hut. The old man fell backward, crying that he had only asked for some food to eat. "I am tired, so tired," said the old man. "I will wait here. Bring the food to me if you have pity on me, daughter, or leave me to die."

Holding the bowl of rice in one hand and the pot of water in the other, Sita bowed her head in shame. "It's only a tired, hungry old man," she thought, "how can I not help him?" And with that thought, she stepped outside the circle. In a flash, the old man turned into Ravana the Demon King. He grabbed Sita by her wrist, dragged her into his winged chariot and flew off into the sky. The sun, which had shone so gently, suddenly clouded over and darkness fell upon Dandaka Forest.

Ravana's chariot rose higher and higher through the dark clouds. As it sped toward his palace in Lanka, a huge vulture flew up to challenge its driver. This was Jatayu, King of the Birds, whose wings ran the length of the sky. With just the tip of one wing, Jatayu lashed out at the chariot, forcing Ravana to slow down.

There followed a great battle, for Ravana had drawn his mighty sword. Jatayu fought fiercely, trying to make Ravana give Sita back.

"Do not harm Sita!" he thundered. "Release her or
you will die, for you have no right to carry her away from
here!" Ravana took no notice. Then, with his wings spread out
wide, Jatayu swooped once more — but the King of the Demons
quickly slashed Jatayu's wings. One! Two! The battle was over.
Without his wings, the great Jatayu fell slowly from the sky,
down, down, through the dark clouds. Ravana laughed
horribly as he continued his journey to Lanka, with Sita
still his prisoner.

Jatayu fell with a crash into Dandaka Forest, close to Sita's hut. There it was that Rama and Lakshmana came upon the vulture. "Rama, Rama," said the dying Jatayu. "Ravana tricked you with the golden deer and has taken Sita to Lanka. Forgive me, Rama, I could not save her."

"There is nothing to forgive, Jatayu," said Rama. "You have done more than we could. And you have paid a price greater than we would have wished. You will live long in my heart, Jatayu."

Then Jatayu breathed his last breath and died. "I should never have left her!" cursed Lakshmana.

"What is done cannot be undone by words," said Rama. "We must find Sita. Tear down the hut, and we'll set off."

"Can we two, by ourselves, defeat Ravana and his army of demons and win back Sita?" asked Lakshmana.

Rama did not answer. He gathered his weapons and the two brothers began to walk southward through the forest.

For many days and nights the brothers walked, going south, ever southward. One evening, they found themselves walking along a narrow path. Looking ahead, they saw a huge old monkey lying across their path. "We must pay our respects," Rama told Lakshmana.

"Respect? Him?" Lakshmana cried out indignantly.

"Yes," said Rama, "for this old monkey you see before you can be none other than Hanuman, the God of the Wind."

As soon as Rama said his name, the old monkey vanished, and in his place stood the mighty Hanuman, sixty feet tall and carrying a huge golden mace. Hanuman knelt on one knee and, pressing his palms together, bowed before Rama. "It is not for Rama and Lakshmana to bow before Hanuman, but for Hanuman to pay his respects to the great Princes of Ayodhya! Forgive me for my little trick, but I wanted to make sure you were indeed Rama and Lakshmana and not some demons in disguise. But tell me, what are you doing here?"

Then the brothers told him all that had happened to them, and that they were going to Lanka to bring back their Sita. "You have a long journey ahead of you," Hanuman told them, "for Ravana's kingdom in Lanka is an island that lies miles away from the edge of the forest, surrounded by deep ocean. Perhaps I can make your search easier. Come, I will take you both to the edge of the forest, so you can see for yourselves." So saying, Hanuman lifted Rama and Lakshmana onto his shoulders, jumped high into the sky and flew like the wind to the edge of Dandaka Forest.

When they reached the edge of the forest, they could all see the island of Lanka in the far distance, with the roaring sea between them. Fires burned all over the island, and smoke rose high from these fires, clouding the light of the sun. Rama was at a loss: "How can we get across?" he asked out loud. "And how can the two of us take on the ten thousand demons of Ravana's army?"

By way of an answer, Hanuman whistled out loud, and the sound was like the crack of thunder. A moment later, from the shore behind them, there arose a noise like waves in the sea, getting louder as it grew nearer. Soon, lined up on the shore, there stood thousands and thousands of monkeys. "Here," said Hanuman, "is the answer to both your worries! Our Monkey Army will gather all the stones from Dandaka Forest and build a bridge across the sea. We shall use big stones, small stones, any stones we can find, and we shall join this place marked by your feet with the island that lies smoking on the horizon!"

And so Hanuman and his Monkey Army began to work, building their bridge over the ocean to Lanka. Seven times the sun rose in the east and sank in the west, and on the eighth day, the bridge was complete.

The Monkey Army, with Rama, Lakshmana and Hanuman at its head, crossed the bridge into Lanka. Before them and around them and above them were thousands and thousands of demons. The demons hurled spears filled with smoke; they carved out hillsides and threw down tons of earth; their axes tore into the Monkey Army. But Rama and Lakshmana fired arrow upon arrow — arrows carrying fire, arrows carrying lightning, arrows that built huge walls protecting the Monkey Army. And their arrows stung the demons, cutting off their heads, arms and legs. Demon after demon came crashing to the earth. Very soon, a huge pile of corpses lay at Rama and Lakshmana's feet. It seemed that all the demons that had ever frightened anyone in the world were dying, so fierce was the battle.

At last, Ravana came out of his palace. "Come and fight me, Rama, fight me if you dare! I will not fall as easily as my demons. Sita is mine, and from this day, when I finally kill you, this world will know only darkness. Dark clouds will bring smiles to people's faces, and they will hide from the sun! Come and fight me!"

Before Rama could take up the challenge, Lakshmana put an arrow in his bow and let it fly at the sneering Ravana. The sharp blade cut off Ravana's head — but as soon as it fell to the ground, another one grew in its place! Lakshmana fired arrow upon arrow — nine times he shot Ravana and cut off his head, and nine times a new head arose, laughing so loud the earth shook to the skies. "What is happening, Rama?" asked Lakshmana.

"Is that the best you can do?" shouted Ravana. "Is this the limit of your power to save Sita? Don't hide behind your brother, Rama, come out and face me alone.

When he heard Ravana's boasts, Rama blazed with fury. Wild flames danced on his skin, and his eyes gleamed as he stooped to place an arrow in his great bow. Just then, Hanuman came up to him. "Rama," murmured Hanuman, "you are mistaken if you think Ravana's power lies in his head. Aim your arrow — the arrow you won long ago in King Janaka's palace — aim that arrow into Ravana's stomach, for that is where the seat of his power lies."

Then Rama calmed himself, bowed in prayer before his arrow and, stringing it to his bow, let it fly. And as the arrow sped through the sky

from Rama's bow, it seemed that time itself had slowed down. The armies of demons and monkeys stood still, watching the arrow slowly travel to its target. Ravana stood still, seeing the arrow come toward him in slow motion. No wind blew, no sound could be heard, no one dared to breathe. The arrow struck Ravana in the center of his stomach. His face was filled with surprise and pain. And then, very slowly, he began to sink to the ground and lay down, very still. Silence fell on the battlefield. The battle was over.

Then Sita came out of Lanka. As she walked toward Rama, her gentle face bright with love, all the monkeys bowed to her. They knelt around her in a circle, and none of them moved. Breaking the silence, Rama ordered Lakshmana, "Bring clothes fit for a queen. Today Sita is to become queen again, her hand in my right hand!"

Sita gently closed her eyes. "How long have I waited to hear those words," she sighed, "and feel the touch of your hand in mine."

And as Rama and Sita embraced, the fires burning in Lanka began to die out. The wind began to blow, carrying the smoke before it. From the sky, piercing the dark clouds, there began to fall tiny lights — flickering oil lamps, lying in clay dishes. Soon, hundreds and thousands of these lights filled the sky, banishing the dark clouds, and the heavens were bright again.

Rama turned to Sita and said, "Let us leave this palace of demons."

"Yes," replied Sita, "and return to the forest of Dandaka."

"No," said Rama, "fourteen years have now passed. It is time for us to return to Ayodhya. When you had been stolen by Ravana, my stepbrother Bharata came to the forest and begged me to return and take his place. I told him I would only go back when I had found you, and now I have."

"But how can we make our way back?" asked Sita. "Must we walk back all that way?"

"That will not be necessary," said a familiar voice, and Hanuman bowed before Rama, Sita and Lakshmana. "Come, climb on my shoulders and soon we will be above Ayodhya, the home you left fourteen years ago!" And so saying, Hanuman lifted the three of them into the sky and sailed across the heavens.

By the time they neared Ayodhya, night had fallen. Sita suddenly cried out, "Rama look — look below! All those shining lights! It's as if the stars have moved from the heavens above to the Earth below!"

"Fair Sita," Hanuman explained, "your return is not a surprise to the citizens of Ayodhya. They have all lit oil lamps in their windows to celebrate your homecoming, and to honor their new king and queen. Ayodhya rejoices, and every man, woman, child and elder welcomes you. The vaults full of ghee and butter are open, the fountains are sparkling. The flowers are in full bloom, and the musicians are ready, for tonight will be a special night for everyone alive."

"Divaali," murmured Rama.

"Divaali?" queried Sita.

"A festival of lights," said Rama. "Henceforth, for all time to come, this night will be remembered in just this way all over the world — the night that Rama and Sita returned home!"

Then Hanuman landed in the palace courtyard among the joyful citizens of Ayodhya and everyone burst into song. And when Rama, Sita and Lakshmana felt again the earth of their home beneath their feet, night suddenly turned to day and from the shining sun, it seemed, hundreds and thousands of sweet-smelling jasmine petals fell down to Earth.

# ✿ ✿ ✿ *The Festival of Divaali* ✿ ✿ ✿

*D*ivaali is modern India's national festival, similar to Christmas in the West. While essentially a Hindu festival, in India it is not uncommon to find Muslims, Sikhs, Buddhists and Christians also taking part. Typically, the festival is marked in each household by small oil lamps (called "diva" in Hindi) lined up on window ledges and along doorways. Firework displays have become necessary accompaniments to the festival, rockets and sparklers being the most common. Divaali is also a social occasion, when gifts and sweet-meats are exchanged between families, relatives and friends. In Indian cities, and wherever else in the world that Indians live, Divaali continues to turn night into day, with electric light bulbs replacing divas where necessary.

Also, since Sita is a manifestation of Lakshmi, the goddess of wealth, Divaali is the occasion for businessmen and women to do their accounts, hoping that Sita/Lakshmi will grace them in the year to come! Those who have no businesses to do the accounts for mark the festival by gambling! It is especially considered bad luck to turn away a stranger who comes to the door during Divaali.

In many parts of northern India, Divaali is also the occasion for a particular form of street theater, called "Raam-Lila" (literally, the "Play of Rama"). Local children and adults often prepare throughout the year for this reenactment of the story of Rama and Sita. Elaborate costumes are made and sets erected, transforming local sites into settings for the Divaali story. Typically, children are chosen to play Rama, Sita and Lakshmana and, throughout the period of the presentation, these children are revered by all as the incarnations of these three gods.

The story of Divaali, *The Ramayana,* has been handed down through the oral tradition for many centuries, with numerous variants and subthemes surrounding the central plot. Like any son or daughter of India, my introduction to this great epic was through my parents. My father shared the adventures of Rama and Sita with me when I was a child, and his influence was reinforced by my mother's frequent recitations of the version that is best-known in India today — that of the fifteenth-century Hindu poet, Tulsidass. It is on this version that my retelling is based.

*Jatinder Verma*

Divaali is pronounced Div-AA-li and can be spelt in any of the following ways: Divaali, Divali, Diwali.

# Barefoot Books
### Celebrating Art and Story

At Barefoot Books, we celebrate art and story with books that open the hearts and minds of children from all walks of life, inspiring them to read deeper, search further, and explore their own creative gifts. Taking our inspiration from many different cultures, we focus on themes that encourage independence of spirit, enthusiasm for learning, and acceptance of other traditions. Thoughtfully prepared by writers, artists, and storytellers from all over the world, our products combine the best of the present with the best of the past to educate our children as the caretakers of tomorrow.

*www.barefootbooks.com*